Anansi and the Talking Melon

retold by Eric A. Kimmel
illustrated by Janet Stevens

SILVER BURDETT GINN

Needham, MA   Parsippany, NJ
Atlanta, GA   Deerfield, IL   Irving, TX   Santa Clara, CA

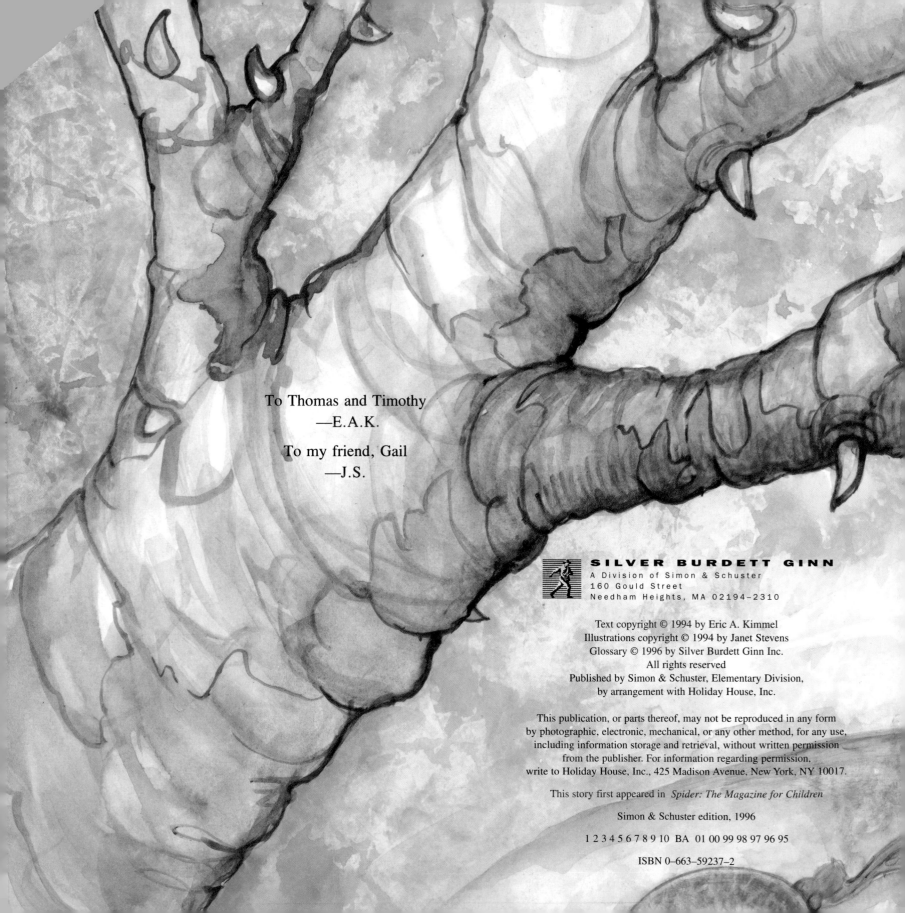

To Thomas and Timothy
—E.A.K.

To my friend, Gail
—J.S.

SILVER BURDETT GINN
A Division of Simon & Schuster
160 Gould Street
Needham Heights, MA 02194–2310

Text copyright © 1994 by Eric A. Kimmel
Illustrations copyright © 1994 by Janet Stevens
Glossary © 1996 by Silver Burdett Ginn Inc.
All rights reserved
Published by Simon & Schuster, Elementary Division,
by arrangement with Holiday House, Inc.

This story first appeared in *Spider: The Magazine for Children*

Simon & Schuster edition, 1996

1 2 3 4 5 6 7 8 9 10 BA 01 00 99 98 97 96 95

ISBN 0–663–59237–2

One fine morning Anansi the Spider sat high up in a thorn tree looking down into Elephant's garden. Elephant was hoeing his melon patch. The ripe melons seemed to call out to Anansi, ''Look how juicy and sweet we are! Come eat us!''

Anansi loved to eat melons, but he was much too lazy to grow them himself. So he sat up in the thorn tree, watching and waiting, while the sun rose high in the sky and the day grew warm. By the time noon came, it was too hot to work. Elephant put down his hoe and went inside his house to take a nap.

Here was the moment Anansi had been waiting for. He broke off a thorn and dropped down into the melon patch. He used the thorn to bore a hole in the biggest, ripest melon.

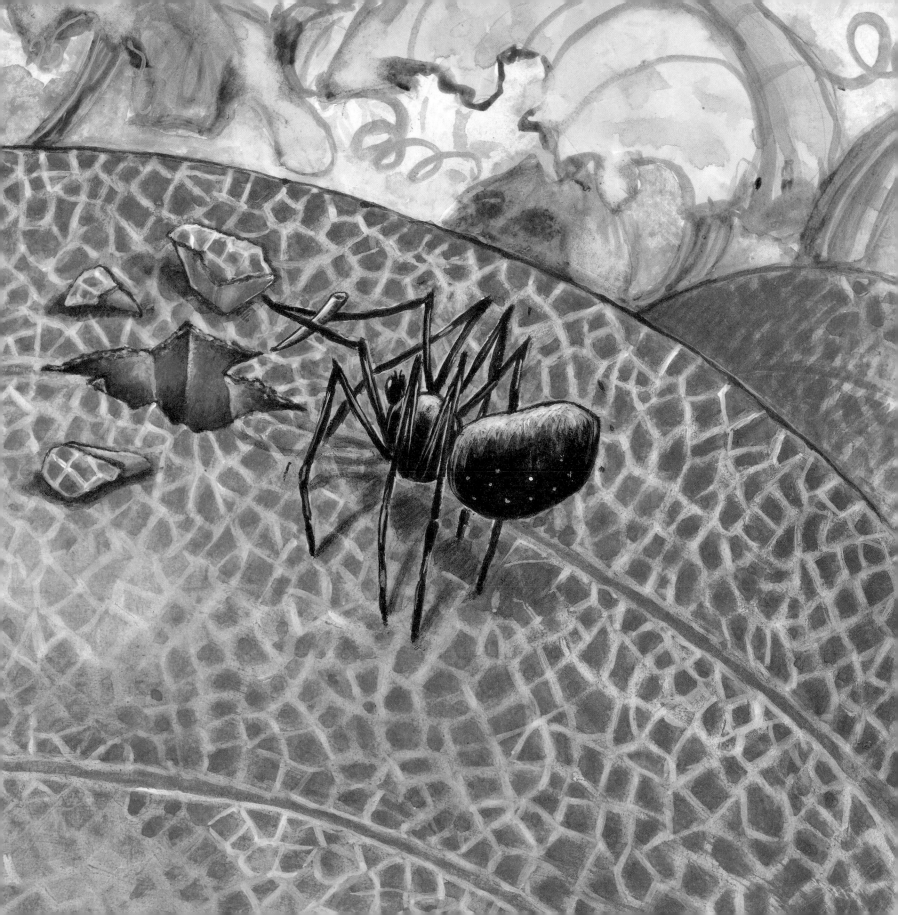

Anansi squeezed inside and started eating. He ate and ate until he was as round as a berry.

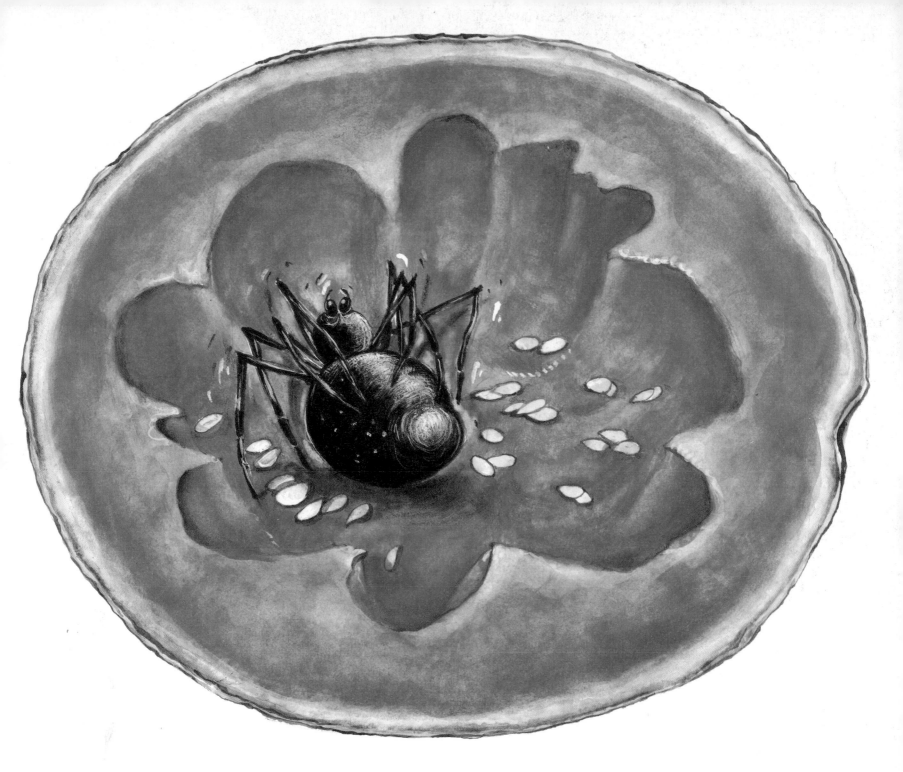

"I'm full," Anansi said at last. "Elephant will be coming back soon. It is time to go."

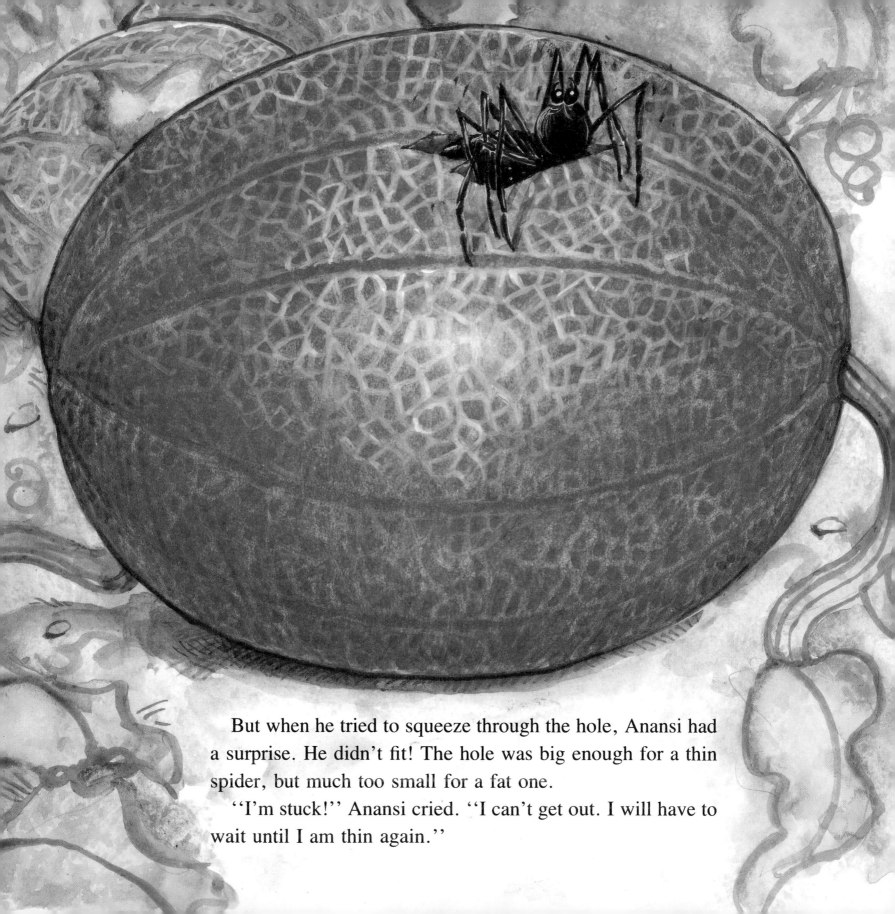

But when he tried to squeeze through the hole, Anansi had a surprise. He didn't fit! The hole was big enough for a thin spider, but much too small for a fat one.

"I'm stuck!" Anansi cried. "I can't get out. I will have to wait until I am thin again."

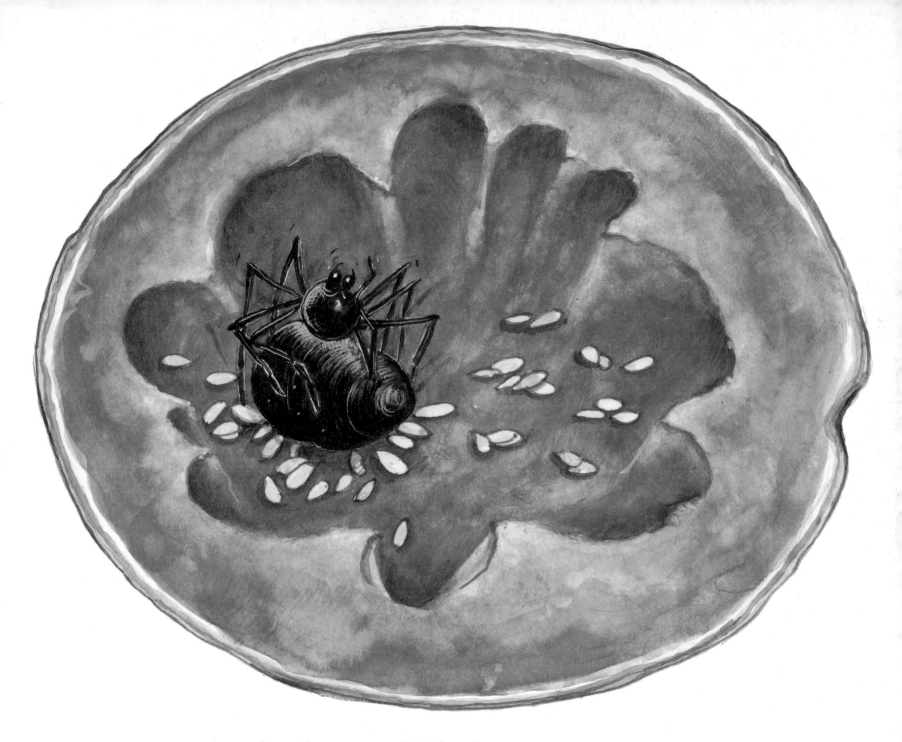

Anansi sat down on a pile of melon seeds and waited to get thin. Time passed slowly.

"I'm bored," Anansi said. "I wish I had something to do."

Just then he heard Elephant returning to the garden. Anansi had an idea. ''When Elephant gets closer, I will say something. Elephant will think the melon is talking. What fun!''

Elephant walked over to the melon patch. ''Look at this fine melon. How big and ripe it is!'' he said, picking it up.

"Ouch!" cried Anansi.
Elephant jumped. "Aah! Who said that?"

"I did. The melon," Anansi said.

"I didn't know melons could talk," said Elephant.

"Of course we do. We talk all the time. The trouble is, you never listen."

"I can't believe my ears!" Elephant exclaimed. "A talking melon! Who could believe it? I must show this to the king."

Elephant ran down the road, carrying the melon with Anansi inside. Along the way, he ran into Hippo.

''Where are you going with that melon?'' Hippo asked.

''I'm taking it to the king,'' Elephant told him.

''What for? The king has hundreds of melons.''

''He doesn't have one like this,'' Elephant said. ''This is a talking melon.''

Hippo didn't believe Elephant. ''A talking melon? What an idea! That's as ridiculous as . . .''

". . . a skinny hippo," the melon said.

Hippo got so angry his face turned red. "Who said that? Did you say that, Elephant?"

"It wasn't me. It was the melon," Elephant said. "I told you it talks. Do you believe me now?"

"I do!" Hippo exclaimed. "I want to go with you. I want to hear what the king says when you show him this talking melon."

"Come along, then," said Elephant. So Elephant and Hippo went down the road together, carrying the melon.

By and by, they ran into Warthog. "Where are you taking that melon?" Warthog asked them.

"We're taking it to the king," Elephant and Hippo told him.

"What for? The king has hundreds of melons," Warthog said.

"He doesn't have one like this," Hippo replied. "This melon talks. I heard it."

Warthog started to laugh. "A talking melon? Why, that's as ridiculous as . . ."

". . . a handsome warthog," said the melon.

Warthog got so angry he shook all over. "Who said that? Did you say that, Elephant? Did you say that, Hippo?"

"Of course not!" Hippo and Elephant told him. "The melon talks. Do you believe us now?"

"I do!" cried Warthog. "Let me go with you. I want to see what the king does when you show him this talking melon."

So Warthog, Elephant, and Hippo went down the road together, carrying the melon.

Along the way, they met Ostrich, Rhino, and Turtle. They didn't believe the melon could talk either until they heard it for themselves. Then they wanted to come along too.

The animals came before the king. Elephant bowed low as he placed the melon at the king's feet.

The king looked down. "Why did you bring me a melon?" he asked Elephant. "I have hundreds of melons growing in my garden."

"You don't have one like this," Elephant said. "This melon talks."

"A talking melon? I don't believe it. Say something, Melon." The king prodded the melon with his foot.

The melon said nothing.

"Melon," the king said in a slightly louder voice, "there is no reason to be shy. Say whatever you like. I only want to hear you talk."

The melon still said nothing. The king grew impatient.

"Melon, if you can talk, I want you to say something. I command you to speak."

The melon did not make a sound.

The king gave up. "Oh, this is a stupid melon!" he said.

Just then the melon spoke. "Stupid, am I? Why do you say that? I'm not the one who talks to melons!"

The animals had never seen the king so angry. "How dare this melon insult me!" he shouted. The king picked up the melon and hurled it as far as he could.

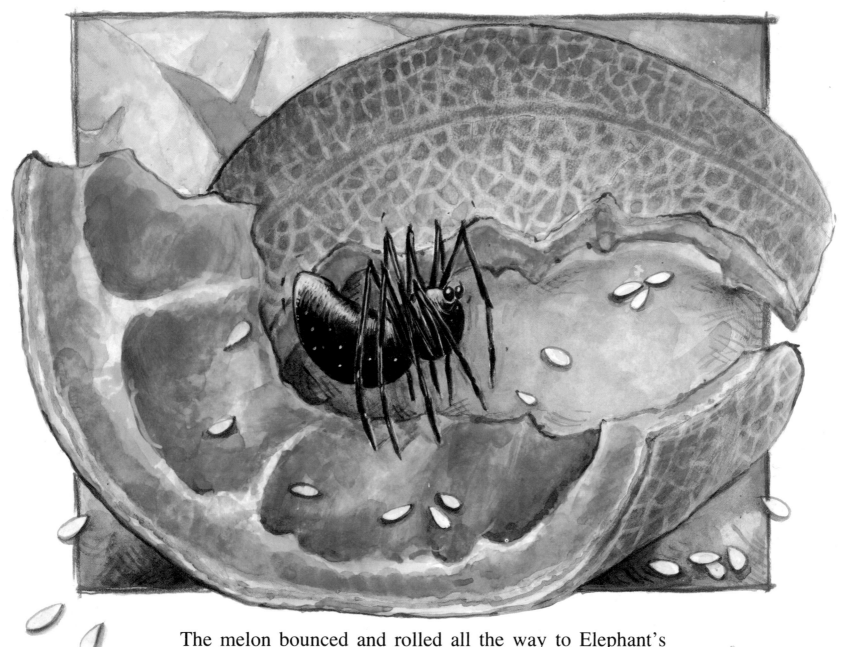

The melon bounced and rolled all the way to Elephant's house. KPOM! It smacked into the thorn tree and burst into pieces. Anansi picked himself up from among the bits of melon rind.

All the excitement had made him thin. And now that he was thin again, he was hungry. Anansi climbed the banana tree. He settled himself in the middle of a big bunch of bananas and started eating.

Elephant returned. He went straight to the melon patch.

"You melons got me in trouble with the king!" Elephant said. "From now on, you can talk all you like. I'm not going to listen to a word you say!"

"Good for you, Elephant!" Anansi called from the bananas. "We bananas should have warned you. Talking melons are nothing but trouble."

Glossary

bore (bôr) *v.* To make a hole by digging or drilling. *She uses her pencil to bore a hole in the cardboard.*

bored (bôrd) *adj.* Not interested. *He is tired and bored because he has nothing to do.*

bow (bou) *v.* To bend down the head and body to show respect. *They bow down low when the king comes by.*

com·mand (kə mand´) *v.* To give an order. *The leaders command the people to start marching.*

ex·claim (ek sklām´) *v.* To speak out suddenly with excitement or strong feeling. *"I can win!" the girl would exclaim before every race.*

hand·some (han´ səm) *adj.* Nice to look at. Good-looking. *Everyone says the boy looks handsome in his new cap.*

hoe (hō) *v.* To dig in dirt with a tool having a flat blade and long handle. *She likes to hoe in the garden and dig up the weeds.*

hurl (hʉl) *v.* To throw with great force. *They hurl the ball back and forth across the yard.*

im•pa•tient (im pā′ shənt) *adj.* Tired of waiting. *The children became impatient when the play didn't start.*

in•sult (in sult′) *v.* To say something that hurts a person's feelings. *They don't want to insult the cook by saying the food isn't good.*

mel•on (mel′ ən) *n.* A large, juicy fruit filled with seeds that grows on a vine. *Let's have fresh melon for dessert.*

patch (pach) *n.* A small piece of land used as a garden. *The chipmunks ate the berries in the strawberry patch.*

prod (präd) *v.* To poke at something with a finger, foot, or pointed object. *She uses a stick to prod the mud from her shoe.*

ri•dic•u•lous (ri dik′ yə ləs) *adj.* Foolish or silly. *It looks ridiculous when people wear their shirts inside out.*

rind (rīnd) *n.* A hard outer layer. *She cuts through the orange rind and the juice comes out.*

thorn (thôrn) *n.* A short, sharp point growing out of a plant. *Her finger hurt when she touched the thorn on the rosebush.*

warn (wôrn) *v.* To tell someone to be careful. *The mother tries to warn her child about watching out for cars before crossing the street.*